The Adventures of George the germ

Written by
Heidi Meadows, RN

Illustrated by
Emma Shull

Published by Orange Hat Publishing 2021
ISBN 9781645382157

Copyrighted © 2021 by Heidi Meadows, RN
All Rights Reserved
The Adventures of George the germ: What are germs?
Written by Heidi Meadows, RN
Illustrated by Emma Shull

All Rights Reserved. Written permission must be secured from the publisher to use or reproduce any part of this book, except for brief quotations in critical reviews or articles.

  For information, please contact:
  Orange Hat Publishing
  www.orangehatpublishing.com
  Waukesha, WI

*This book is not suggesting any medical advice but serves as a reminder for kids to practice healthy habits.

*Contact your pediatrician for any questions regarding your child showing signs or symptoms of getting sick!

*For more guidelines, healthy habits, and ways to prevent the spread of sickness, visit https://www.cdc.gov/ (Center for Disease Control) or https://www.hhs.gov/ (U.S. Department of Health & Human Services).

A special dedication to
our family and friends for much support and encouragement.

A special recognition to
my colleagues at St. Joseph Hospital, Orange, Calif.

A special thanks to
ALL ESSENTIAL workers who are vital in the fight against sickness!

Germs...what are germs?

Germs can give us a headache, a tummy ache, a sore throat, a cough, a stuffy, drippy, tickly nose, body aches, a fever... and more! Germs can make us SICK!!!

How do we live with germs? Our bodies have ways to keep us well, but sometimes there are just too many germs, and we get sick. Remembering to do these healthy habits can help keep germs away!

Germs are everywhere, yet they are too small for us to see. Since they are too small to see, it is easy for us to forget about them.

LOOK inside the circle below...
Can you find any germs?

Let us look through this microscope and see if we can find anything in the circle now. Why, there is George the germ with his germ buddies!!!

So, let's pretend we are just as small as George the germ and his germ buddies and find out how their adventure began. Look...it started when they were playing on the hand of a little boy named Dustin. Let's watch what happened next.

Dustin was not feeling well. He woke up with a stuffy, drippy, tickly nose. As his nose began to drip, Dustin took the hand that George the germ and his germ buddies were on and wiped his nose. The germs tumbled into what they thought was a big cave.

George the germ and his germ buddies could feel something soft and tickly touching them. They turned on their bump-lights so they could see what was going on!

There are tiny hairs in the nose that stop dust and dirt from getting into our bodies. The germs thought the nose hairs were ropes and started climbing and swinging on them.

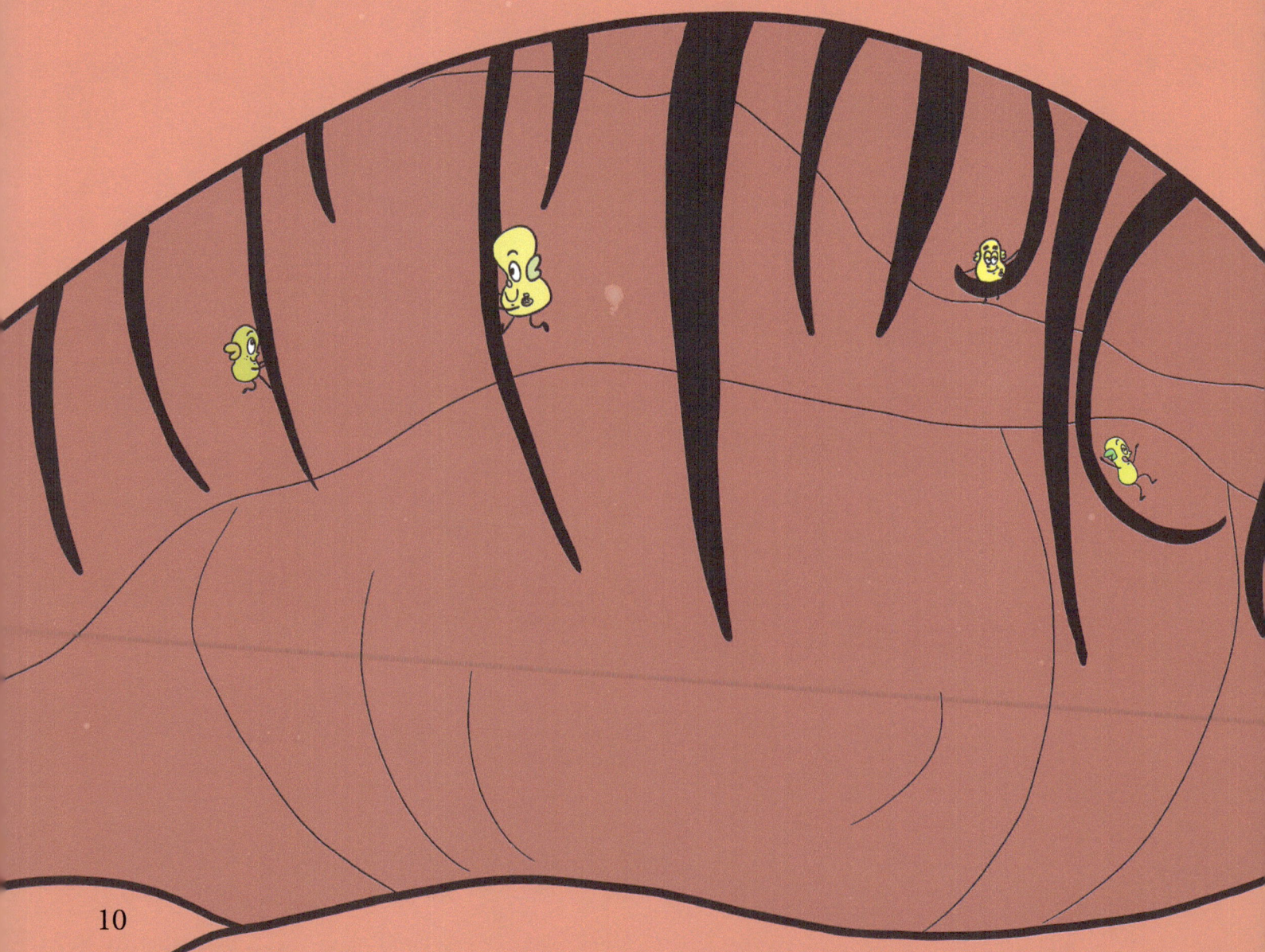

At first the hairs were sticky, so it was easy for the germs to go up and down, but over time, the ropes became wet and slippery, making them much too hard to play on. George the germ and his germ buddies decided to go deeper into the cave.

As they went farther back into Dustin's nose, they came to a soft, spongy, upside-down hill. If we were to look inside a nose, the soft, spongy, upside-down hill is actually a small lump, called the adenoid. There are two adenoids way in the back of the nose, one on either side.

George the germ and his germ buddies were ready to have some fun sliding down the upside-down hill. Holding onto each other, one in front of the other, they made a germ train and off they went! But then suddenly, the germs had to stop.

Out of nowhere, the upside-down hill came to an end. All the germs could see was a giant hole and then another, much bigger hill across the way. The germs did not know they were looking down into Dustin's throat, and the hill they saw past the giant hole was one of Dustin's tonsils.

Just like the adenoids in the nose, there are two lumps called tonsils in the back of the throat. Both the adenoids and tonsils fight illness. Sometimes, when we become sick, they can grow bigger and become painful in the nose and throat.

The germs knew a fun game called "You got Me," which would close the giant hole by causing the upside-down hill to grow bigger, making it safe for them to slide to the next big hill. As they began, the germs took turns answering silly questions. The germ that got the most right, took a piece of a special string and pushed it into the spongy upside-down hill.

George the germ won the first game, so he pushed a piece of his string into the spongy upside-down hill. At that moment, out popped another germ that looked just like him, and the upside-down hill grew a little bigger! George the germ yelled, "You got ME!"

Hour after hour, as time went on, the germs played their game. The hill kept growing bigger and bigger, and there were a lot of new germ friends to play with, many that looked just like George the germ and his germ buddies.

Finally, the upside-down hill had gotten so big, the germs saw they could get to the other side with no worries. All the germs, including George the germ and his germ buddies, began forming their germ trains.

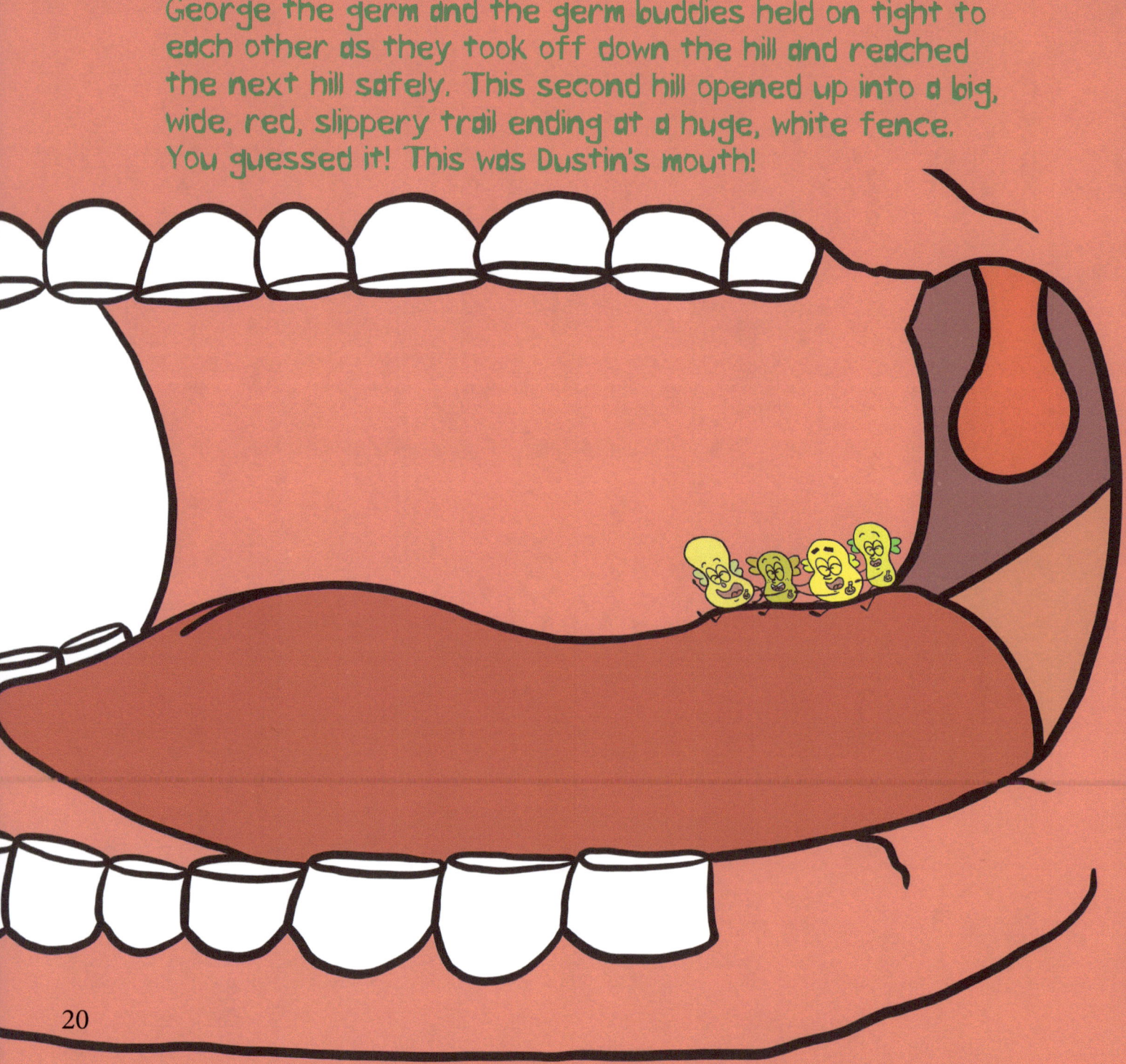

George the germ and the germ buddies held on tight to each other as they took off down the hill and reached the next hill safely. This second hill opened up into a big, wide, red, slippery trail ending at a huge, white fence. You guessed it! This was Dustin's mouth!

The germs were having so much fun! They had no idea they were making Dustin's throat hurt and causing him to sneeze and cough. Even though he did not feel well, Dustin left for school so that he could be with his best friend, Randy.

When Dustin got to his classroom, he sat down at his desk next to his best friend, Randy. He took off his mask to say hi, but he accidentally let out a huge sneeze! Randy pulled down his mask to tell Dustin quietly to put his mask back on. The class had just been told they needed to wear them.

Right as Dustin sneezed, George the germ and his germ buddies had just finished climbing to the top of the upside-down hill again, waiting for their turn to go down. A huge gust of wind picked up George the germ and off he went... right out of Dustin's mouth.

The wind pushed George the germ's buddies so hard, they rolled and rolled and rolled, all the way back to the opening of the cave. Dustin quickly wiped his nose with his hand and then gave Randy a fist-bump, tumbling the germs onto Randy's hand.

Randy could see that his friend was not feeling well. With his mask still pulled down, Randy asked what he could do to help. As Randy spoke, George the germ was floating by his germ buddies, laughing and waving. George did not realize that the bubble he was on was just about to go into Randy's mouth.

The germ buddies turned off their bump-lights and began thinking of ways they could get to their friend.

So... where did George the germ go? Why, he went off on another adventure, of course!

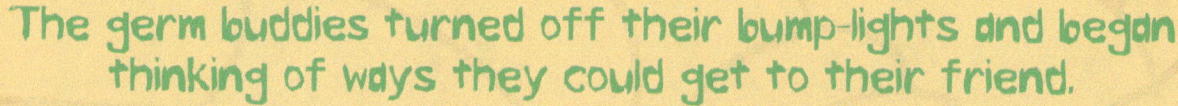

The End

No, this is just the beginning!

As we read each episode of *The Adventures of George the germ*, we learn about germs, how important it is to remember healthy habits, AND ways to help prevent you and others from getting sick! Being sick stinks, so take care of yourself!

Just remember: spread the word, not the germs!

Awareness + Healthy habits = Prevention

Just remember: spread the word, not the germs.
Reviewing healthy habits from Book 1

1. When Dustin sneezed, George the germ floated out of Dustin's mouth and was headed towards Randy's mouth!

Rule #1. If you do not have a mask, make sure to cover your mouth with your hand, a tissue, or the bend of your elbow when you cough or sneeze, and remember to wash your hands well afterward.

2. When the boys gave each other a fist-bump, the germ buddies tumbled from Dustin's hand to Randy's hand.

Rule #2. Keep your hands clean. Wash your hands with soap and water for at least twenty seconds. (Sing the Happy Birthday song two times!) Be sure to wash the top of your hands, in between your fingers, and the palms as well. Wash frequently, and use hand sanitizer in between!

3. Dustin wiped his nose with his hand.

Rule #3. Do not touch your face! Germs can enter through your nose, eyes, or mouth and get you sick!

4. Dustin did not feel well but still went to school even though he was sick, spreading the germs to his friends.

Rule # 4. Stay home from school when you do not feel well, so you do not get others sick!

5. Dustin's desk is right next to his friend. He sneezed without his mask on and did not cover his mouth, spreading his germs to Randy.

Rule #5. Social Distancing: Keep 3 - 6 feet between you and someone else. Do this especially when you are sick so your germs do not travel to others and get them sick.

Printed in the USA
CPSIA information can be obtained
at www.ICGtesting.com
JSHW070813230324
59717JS00001B/1